THE MAN
WHO TOOK THE INDOORS OUT

ARNOLD LOBEL

Harper & Row, Publishers
New York, Evanston, San Francisco, London

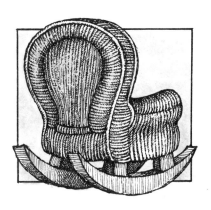

for Adam

There was an old man
Who was named Bellwood Bouse.
He loved all the things
In his very large house.
At the start of each day,
With a duster and broom,
He carefully cleaned
Every well-furnished room.

In his white wicker rocker,
Outdoors in the air,
Bellwood said to himself,
"Now it does not seem fair.
While I sit out here
In the clear morning light,
My wonderful things
Are inside and shut tight.
It does not seem good
And it does not seem kind,
But I have an astounding idea
In my mind."

Bellwood went to the door
And he opened it wide.
He shouted, "Now, Indoors—
Please come outside!"
There was one little sound
From the end of the hall,
Then a hundred small creakings
Behind every wall.
A rolling and rumbling noise
Left no doubt
That everything Indoors
Was on its way out.

The sofa, the footstool,
The tables and chairs,
The lamps and the pictures,
The pillows in pairs.
The drawers with their dresser,
The mirrors and drapes,
An upright piano,
A bunch of wax grapes.
The bed and the quilt
And the clocks, one by one,
Bounced out of the house
In the warm noonday sun.
The cups and the platters,
The spoons and the bowls,
A cookie jar filled up
With cinnamon rolls.
The ladles and pots
And the kettle for tea,
A sink and a stove
That had set themselves free.
The broom and the duster—
All this and much more
Came leaping and tumbling
Out through the door.

The old man exclaimed,
"What a jubilant day!
We will have a parade—
Bellwood Bouse shows the way!"
A preposterous
Sort of procession began.

Some things went skipping,
And other things ran
Through the forests and fields
All that fine afternoon,
While the upright piano
Was playing a tune.

They marched to the village,
And when they were there,
They danced in a circle
Around the town square.
The folk came to watch
In a curious crowd.
They giggled and chuckled,
They laughed long and loud.
"Three cheers for old Bouse!"
Someone said with a shout,
"The man who has taken
The Indoors out!"

On and on went the Indoors
With Bouse in the lead.
But early that evening
Those things gathered speed.
"Do slow down!" Bellwood cried.
"Are we running a race?
I cannot continue
This breathtaking pace."
Still the Indoors rushed on,
Feeling happy and free.
It paid no attention
To old Bellwood's plea.
In a great cloud of dust
It ran far out of sight,
Leaving Bouse all alone
In the darkening night.

The Indoors ran out
To the edge of the land,
Way down near the shore
Where it strolled on the sand.
The sofa and tables,
The bed and the clocks,
Played hide-and-go-seek
On some barnacled rocks.
The pans and the platters,
Each teacup and dish,
Went out for a swim
Like a school of odd fish.
All of Bellwood's possessions,
Well out of his reach,
Watching the waves
Wash the bright moonlit beach.

From deep, wooded valleys
To high mountain peaks,
Bouse called, "Come back, dears!"
For many long weeks.
His coat was in tatters
And wet from the rain.
His cries became echoes,
But all was in vain.
Oh Bellwood, poor Bellwood...
That old man named Bouse,
He gave up the search
And returned to his house.
The white wicker rocker
Was all that he had.
He sat in it feeling
Incredibly sad.

A year passed, and Bouse,
In the blackest of glooms,
Walked up and down
Through his dark, empty rooms.
He climbed to the top
Of his uppermost tower
To watch at the window
For hour after hour.
He said, "How tremendously
Grateful I'd be
If only my Indoors
Would come home to me!"

One morning in winter
Bouse looked down below.
Something was moving
Out there in the snow.
He heard distant music,
A soft, gentle song.
"My piano!" Bouse shouted.
"I could not be wrong!"
As he rushed down the stairs,
Running terribly fast,
He cried, "Has my Indoors
Returned home at last?"

Up the hill to the house
Came a line of lost things.
The kettle was bent,
And the chairs had loose springs.
The mirrors were cracked,
And the teacups were chipped.
The tables were scratched,
And the sofa was ripped.
"Poor dears, you are damaged,"
Said Bouse. "But who cares?
I'm so glad you are back,
I will soon make repairs!"

"I hope," Bellwood said,
"That your journey was fun.
Now come in, for your life
In the outdoors is done."
The exhausted Indoors,
Doing as it was told,

Stumbled into the house
To get out of the cold.
Said Bouse, as he hurried
To lock his front door,
"I will not let my Indoors
Run loose anymore."

And then to his rocker
Bouse made a deep bow.
"White wicker," he said,
"Come and dance with me now."
So there on the slope
Of that snow-covered hill,
In spite of the blizzard,
Ignoring the chill...

The rocker danced
All around and about
With the man who had taken
The Indoors out.